Canyons

by
Gary Paulsen

Teacher Guide

Written by
Phyllis Green

Note

The Laurel Leaf Contemporary Fiction paperback edition © 1990 was used in preparing this guide. Other editions may yield varying page references.

ISBN 1-56137-4822

Copyright infringement is a violation of Federal Law.

© 1999 by Novel Units, Inc., San Antonio, Texas. All rights reserved. No part of this publication may be reproduced, translated, stored in a retrieval system, or transmitted in ~~copying, recording, or otherwise) without prior written p~~

Photocopying of student worksheets by a classroom teach~~ for his/her own class is permissible. Reproduction of any p~~ ~~tem, by for-profit institutions and tutoring centers, or for~~

Novel Units is a registered trademark of Novel Units, Inc.

Printed in the United States of America.

Table of Contents

Skills and Strategies

Thinking
   Brainstorming, research,
   investigation

Comprehension
   Predicting,
   comparison/contrast

Writing
   Description, summarizing

Vocabulary
   Word mapping, vocabulary
   activities

Listening/Speaking
   Dramatization, reports

Literary Elements
   Story elements, characteriza-
   tion, plot summaries,
   foreshadowing

Summary:
Gary Paulsen's 1990 book intertwines the stories of Coyote Runs, a nineteenth century Apache young man killed on his first raid, and Brennan Cole, a twentieth century teen-age runner. When Brennan discovers Coyote Runs' skull, which never received a proper burial, strange things begin to happen. Brennan is overwhelmed by the "presence" of the skull; he knows he is involved somehow with the skull. John Homesley, Brennan's biology teacher, assists in identification. When Brennan decides he must take the skull to a proper resting place, he is led by unexplainable knowledge of the area and survival in the canyons, a kind of supernatural communication from Coyote Runs.

About the Author:
Gary Paulsen was born in Minneapolis, Minnesota, in 1939. He now lives in Leonard, Minnesota. During Paulsen's growing-up years, he moved many times because his father was in the standing Army.

He has worked as a teacher, field engineer, editor, soldier, actor, director, farmer, rancher, truck driver, trapper, professional archer, migrant farm worker, singer, and sailor.

Without formal writing training, he was hired as an associate editor and learned on the job. He spent about a year editing and considers it the best of all possible ways to learn about writing.

Organization of this Guide:
Comprehension questions, vocabulary words, and plot summaries are provided for every chapter. Supplementary activities are included after every three chapters. Teachers can choose activities with their particular groups in mind.

Vocabulary Approach:
The reading level of *Canyons* is 5. Considering also the content and issues of the story, we have included it with books for grades 7-8.

It is suggested that a portion of the reading instructional time daily be used for vocabulary activities. Vocabulary challenge words are identified chapter-by-chapter. Of particular note in this book are words which have multiple meanings depending upon context, words used in describing the book's setting, and words used by the Apaches.

Selected words with multiple meanings include wash (page 15), chewed (page 21), pack (page 38), rose (page 51), fire (page 63), speakers (page 107), exchange (page 135), reel (page 139), engagement (page 141). Webs or chains can be used to record and differentiate meanings.

Because Brennan is a runner, the author has used many different words for "run" or "running" to distinguish kinds of running. Collect these words on an attribute web. On top of the line, note the word. Below the line, distinguish it from the other terms.

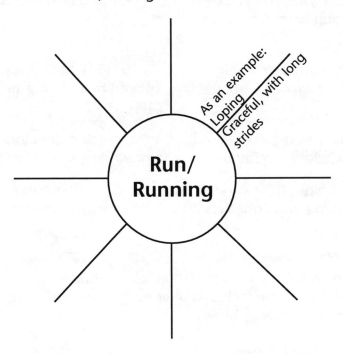

Vocabulary Activities:

1. Draw pictures to remember the word definitions.

2. Try to use the challenge words throughout the day. Underline uses in your work.

3. Create crossword puzzle clues for the words. Quiz classmates.

4. Play Charades to dramatize words.

5. Connect new words to previous knowledge graphically, hooking via meaning, semantic usage, etymology.

6. Vocabulary Definition Bee, Trivial Pursuit, Vocabulary Password—In each of these games, students prepare cards with definitions to use.

Map

Locate El Paso, Texas, Alamogordo Horse Canyon, and Dog Canyon on the map.

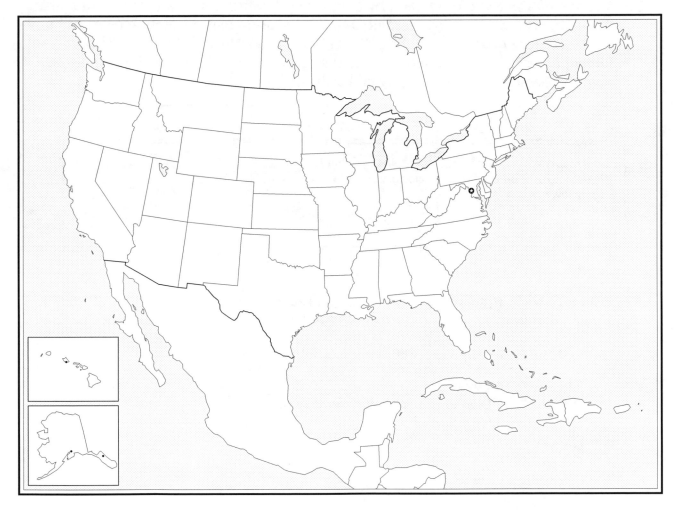

Initiating Activities:
(Several are included from which the teacher can choose for the particular class.)

1. Prepare a framework for reading by completing the first two columns of a modified K-W-L, brainstorming and recording in the **K** column what students *know* about nineteenth century Apaches and about the El Paso, Texas area. In the **W** column, record *student expectations* and *predictions* for the book. The **L** column will be completed after the book is read to record what has been *learned*.

K	W	L
As an example: •*El Paso, Texas is on the Rio Grande River* •*Apaches prized horses*	•*Anti-Anglo feeling by Apaches* •*No cars or speedy travel*	

2. Read a passage from another Gary Paulsen book. Encourage students to sit back and enjoy. Then introduce this Gary Paulsen book for study. Solicit predictions.

   Young adult fiction by Gary Paulsen include the following titles:

   Amos Gets Famous
   The Boy Who Owned the School: A Comedy of Love
   The Case of the Dirty Bird
   The Cookcamp
   The Crossing
   Culpepper's Cannon
   Dancing Carl
   Dogsong (Novel Unit Available)
   Dunc and Amos and the Red Tattoos
   Dunc and Amos Hit the Big Top
   Dunc and the Flaming Ghost
   Dunc and the Scam Artists
   Dunc Breaks the Record
   Dunc Gets Tweaked
   Dunc's Doll
   Dunc's Halloween

The Foxman
Hatchet (Novel Unit Available)
The Haymeadow
The Island
Nightjohn
The River
Sentries
Tracker
The Voyage of the Frog (Novel Unit Available)
The Winter Room
Woodsong (Novel Unit Available)

3. Paulsen's *Canyons* gets very positive reviews.

   "Paulsen involves readers so deeply in the lives of both characters...that the whole becomes a compelling and dramatic experience that is powerful stuff...New and unforgettable."—<u>School Library Journal</u>

   "Readers...will be rewarded with an insightful, sympathetic vignette of the tragic end of a life..."—<u>Kirkus Review</u>

   "[A] deft and thought-provoking adventure novel."—<u>Booklist</u>

   What do you expect from such a book?

4. Look at the cover to collect clues about the book. What objects are pictured? What do you predict?

5. The predominant object and image in this book is a skull. What do you expect? What questions do you have about a skull?

Bulletin Board/Display Suggestions:
1. Develop the comparison between Coyote Runs and Brennan Cole with an extra large Venn diagram or T comparison.

2. Expand the comparison with applications from contemporary student life and world—students from different cultural heritages. The bulletin board is a large web with many ideas, quotations, pictures, etc. about the subject. Then a Venn or T is used to organize and compare.

Using Predictions in the Novel Unit Approach

We all make predictions as we read—little guesses about what will happen next, how the conflict will be resolved, which details given by the author will be important to the plot, which details will help to fill in our sense of a character. Students should be encouraged to predict, to make sensible guesses. As students work on predictions, these discussion questions can be used to guide them: What are some of the ways to predict? What is the process of a sophisticated reader's thinking and predicting? What clues does an author give us to help us in making our predictions? Why are some predictions more likely than others?

A predicting chart is for students to record their predictions. As each subsequent chapter is discussed, you can review and correct previous predictions. This procedure serves to focus on predictions and to review the stories.

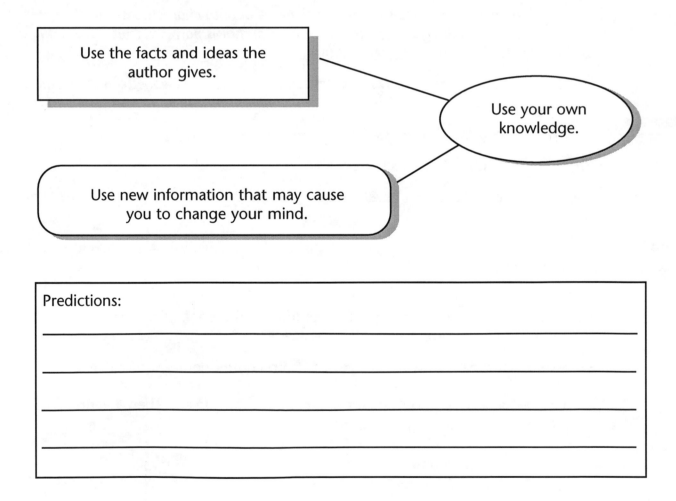

Use the facts and ideas the author gives.

Use your own knowledge.

Use new information that may cause you to change your mind.

Predictions:

_____

_____

_____

_____

Prediction Chart

What characters have we met so far?	What is the conflict in the story?	What are your predictions?	Why did you make those predictions?

Using Character Webs—In the Novel Unit Approach

Attribute Webs are simply a visual representation of a character from the novel. They provide a systematic way for the students to organize and recap the information they have about a particular character. Attribute webs may be used after reading the novel to recapitulate information about a particular character or completed gradually as information unfolds, done individually, or finished as a group project.

One type of character attribute web uses these divisions:

● How a character acts and feels. (How does the character feel in this picture? How would you feel if this happened to you? How do you think the character feels?)

● How a character looks. (Close your eyes and picture the character. Describe him to me.)

● Where a character lives. (Where and when does the character live?)

● How others feel about the character. (How does another specific character feel about our character?)

In group discussion about the student attribute webs and specific characters, the teacher can ask for backup proof from the novel. You can also include inferential thinking.

Attribute webs need not be confined to characters. They may also be used to organize information about a concept, object or place.

Attribute Web

The attribute web below is designed to help you gather clues the author provides about what a character is like. Fill in the blanks with words and phrases which tell how the character acts and looks, as well as what the character says and what others say about him or her.

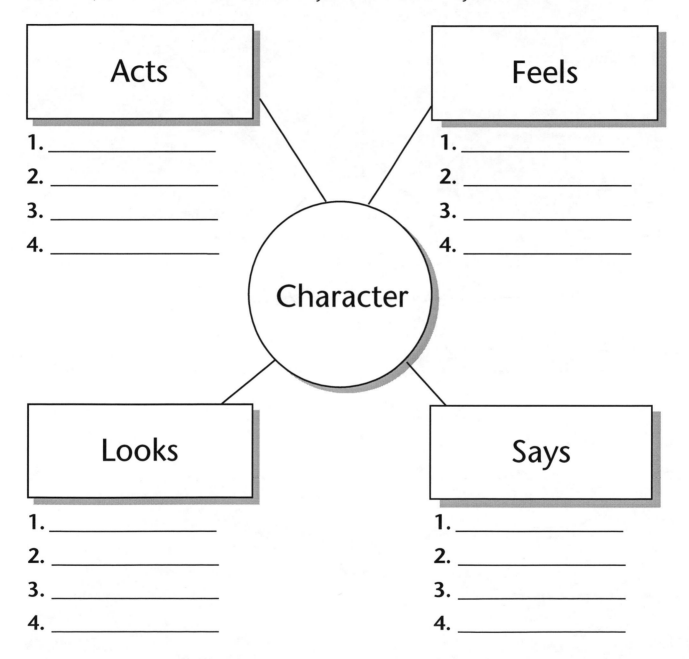

Attribute Web

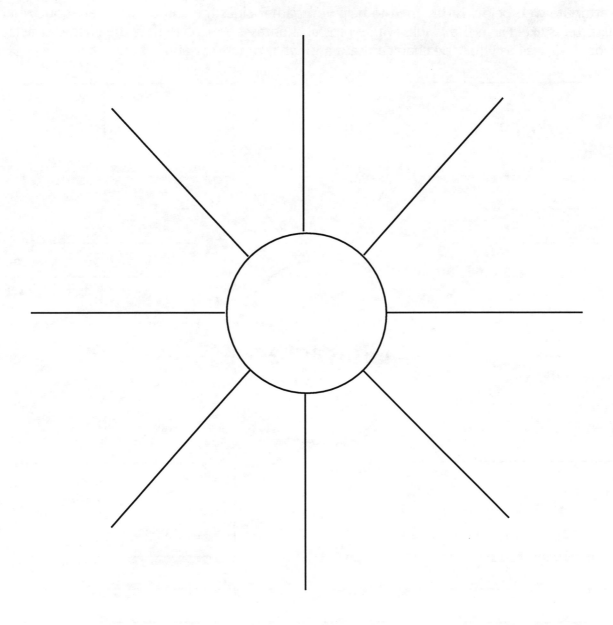

Chapter 1: "Quickening"—Pages 3-6

Plot Summary:
The reader meets Coyote Runs, a young Native American boy, anxious to be accepted as an adult. His friend Magpie reports that he's heard stories that there will be a new raid and Coyote Runs will go along to hold the horses and see how it is to be on a raid.

Vocabulary:

  bluebellies 4   lucifer stick 4

Discussion Questions:
1. Who was Coyote Runs? *(a fourteen-year-old Native American young man who was anticipating keenly his move into manhood)*

2. Why was the word "man" used so many times in this chapter? *(to emphasize Coyote Runs' desire to move from childhood to manhood)*

3. What was the time of the story? How do you know? *(The references to raids and forts suggest nineteenth century times of Indian wars.)*

Chapter 2—Pages 9-13

Plot Summary:
The reader meets Brennan Cole, a teen-ager, who lives in El Paso, Texas.

Discussion Questions:
1. Why doesn't Chapter 2 have a title when Chapter 1 had a title? *(Answers vary, but include idea of uncertainty and need to read more chapters to understand.)*

2. What characters are met in Chapter 2? *(Brennan Cole, Brennan's mother, his mother's friend)* How do you think they'll figure in the story? *(Answers vary.)*

3. What is the importance of the last sentence in the chapter? *(Answers vary, but may reference foreshadowing.)*

Chapter 3: "Dust Spirits"—Pages 15-18

Plot Summary:
Coyote Runs prepares himself for his first raid.

Vocabulary:

  wash 15   goad 18

Discussion Questions:

1. Why was everything perfect in Coyote Runs' view in this chapter? *(He was to go on the next raid, Magpie had lent him a pony, and the spirits of the dust gave him a sign of approval.)*

2. What was the plan for the raid? *(to ride to the low river bank, leave the extra horses with Coyote Runs to watch, and then take horses from the Mexican ranchers)*

3. Consider differing viewpoints. How would the view of horses be different for the Mexican ranchers, the Apaches, the U. S. soldiers? *(ownership and accompanying rights)*

4. What have you learned of Coyote Runs' tribe thus far in the book?

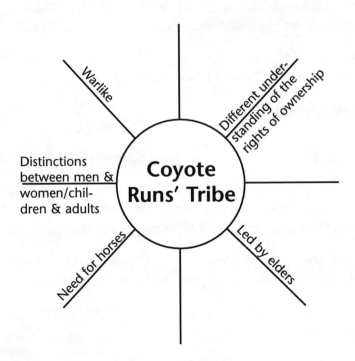

Supplementary Activities:

1. Consider entering adulthood. In small groups brainstorm ways different cultures make the passage. (See graphic on next page.)

Entering Adulthood

- Study and preparation
- More rights and privileges
- Access to adult decisions/councils
- Public acknowledgement (Confirmation)
- Bar Mitzvah or Bat Mitzvah
- Increased responsibility
- Celebration

2. Look for interesting descriptions Gary Paulsen has used in the first three chapters of the book.

   Coyote Runs' mother
   Brennan Cole
   Feelings while running

3. What did Coyote Runs and Magpie learn at the Quaker School? Compare to your schooling.

Quaker School	Your School

Chapter 4—Pages 21-27

Plot Summary:
More detail is given on Brennan's life. His summer job is on a lawn crew.

Vocabulary:
    mesquite 25

Discussion Questions:

1. What is Brennan's summer job? *(as part of Stoney Romero's lawn crew)* Why is it a good job for Brennan? *(It is outside and Stoney asks few questions about Brennan's age.)*

2. Start an attribute web for Brennan.

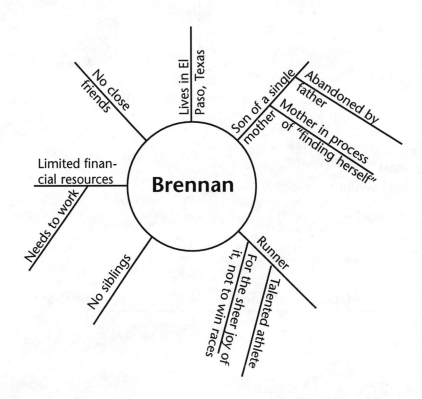

3. How does the author reveal the character of Stoney Romero?

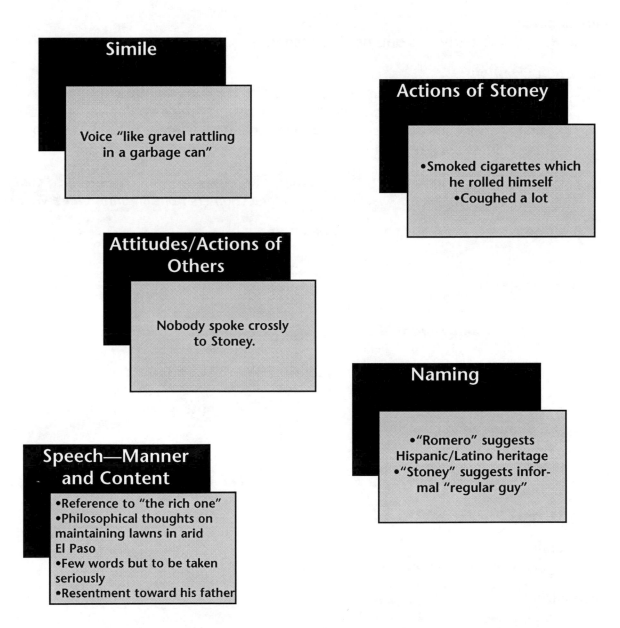

Simile

Voice "like gravel rattling in a garbage can"

Actions of Stoney

• Smoked cigarettes which he rolled himself
• Coughed a lot

Attitudes/Actions of Others

Nobody spoke crossly to Stoney.

Naming

• "Romero" suggests Hispanic/Latino heritage
• "Stoney" suggests informal "regular guy"

Speech—Manner and Content

• Reference to "the rich one"
• Philosophical thoughts on maintaining lawns in arid El Paso
• Few words but to be taken seriously
• Resentment toward his father

4. What is "another relationship" from page 27? What is Brennan's expectation? *(He will have to get to know Bill better, reacting and building a relationship. You can almost feel Brennan's sarcasm in saying "Oh great.")*

Chapter 5: "Nightride"—Pages 29-31

Plot Summary:
The Indian raiding party sets out, riding all night.

Discussion Questions:
1. What was a silliness? What examples did Coyote Runs mention? *(A silliness was a stupid thing to do; eating horse, naming mountains after a pump organ.)* Share other things you'd consider a silliness. Are there cultural differences between your choices for a silliness and those in the book chosen by Coyote Runs? Explain.

2. What was the viewpoint in the chapters with titles? without titles? *(Titled chapters were from Coyote Runs' view and the untitled chapters from Brennan Cole's view.)*

3. Compare Coyote Runs and Brennan Cole.

Coyote Runs	Brennan Cole
•Apache	•Anglo
•Adolescent	•Adolescent
•Wants to be considered an adult	•Wants to be taken seriously
	•Thoughtful

Chapter 6—Pages 33-41

Plot Summary:
Brennan accompanies Bill, his mother, and Bill's youth group on a camping trip.

Vocabulary:
loping 34	bluff 36	yucca 38

Discussion Questions:
1. Explain the phrases (on the next page) from the chapter.

Quotation	Location in Book	Explanation/Meaning
"Sometimes no matter what you do you lose."	Page 34	
"The cards flipped through in his mind."	Page 34	
"...like being in a nest of rats."	Page 35	
"...smooth, dishlike bowls"	Page 38	
"...see what the artist was trying to do with it."	Page 39	
"Some pull, some reaching and pulling thing that made the hair stand up on the back of his neck."	Page 40	

2. How does the scenery of Horse Canyon affect the various members of the camping group?

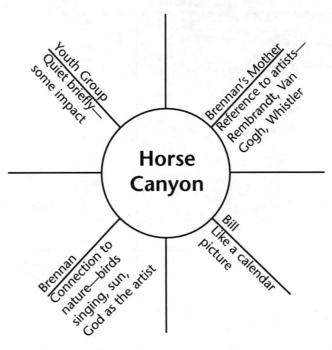

Supplementary Activities:

1. Use the categories from Chapter 4, question 3, to tell about someone you know, either from real life or a book you've read.

2. Investigate the topography of the area around El Paso. Use library and other resources.

3. Collect some photo-pictures worthy of artist status, as described on page 38. What makes a scene special to you? Answer in a short paragraph.

Chapter 7: "Visions"—Pages 43-46

Plot Summary:
Coyote Runs and the Apache raiding party headed by Sancta proceed to the area of El Paso del Norte (the pass of the north) where they camp.

Vocabulary:
> muzzles 43

Discussion Questions:
1. How did the Apache raiding party remain undetected by the soldiers? *(pinched their horses' muzzles so the horses would not make sounds, rode during the night, didn't make large visible fires)*

2. What did the bluebellies do that Coyote Runs might call silliness? *(large fires at night which were easily seen, wore dark wool clothes in summer as well as heavy hats)*

3. What was "hard light"? *(page 46, full daylight)*

Chapter 8—Pages 49-54

Plot Summary:
Brennan and the others reach a camping place. After stories around the fire, including Bill's information about Dog Canyon and the surrounding area, Brennan begins to feel strangely.

Vocabulary:

hyper 49	fire pit 49	stronghold 52
condensing 53		

Discussion Questions:
1. What events from this chapter add to your understanding of the story? *(Bill's information about the Dog Canyon and the earlier Apache involvement connect the two parallel stories in the book.)*

2. What is the source of Brennan's "strange feeling" described at the end of the chapter? *(Answers vary—fear, uncertainty, uneasiness.)*

Chapter 9: "The Raid"—Pages 57-77

Plot Summary:
After a confusing start, Coyote Runs joins the main Apache herd of horses. A large band of soldiers overtake the Apaches and everyone flees. Coyote Runs is shot and then executed when he is discovered hiding beneath a boulder.

Vocabulary:

commotion 58	vaqueros 59	veered 60
faltering 65	bridle 65	reeling 67
lunge 68	betrayal 75	scuffs 76

Discussion Questions:
1. What confused Coyote Runs when he rejoined the raiding party? *(Page 59, The dust and lack of visibility confused him and he initially drove the horses south, instead of north.)*

2. What was the initial assessment of the Apache raid? *(Page 63, "A great raid they would speak of for years around the fire...")*

3. What was the straw horse? *(page 65, the horse Coyote Runs took from the Mexican horses, as his own)*

4. What was Coyote Run's special medicine? *(It was the protection he believed he had from the Dust Spirits. He did escape injury from Mexican guns when he drove the horses the wrong direction.)*

5. How did the chapter end? *(Coyote Runs, after hiding behind a boulder, was executed by the soldiers.)*

6. Compare the beginning, middle, and end of this chapter. How did the emotions vary? How did Paulsen emphasize the feelings and mood?

Time	*Mood*	*Author's Craft*
Beginning	*Hopeful, upbeat*	*Positive words—yes; details*
Middle	*Exuberance, smiling, laughing*	*Detail about new house for Coyote Runs; dialogue*
End	*Death and doom*	*Few words; emphasis on the smells, senses; one word at the conclusion*

Supplementary Activities:
1. How do youngsters and adolescents learn from their elders? Cite some examples from the book and from your own experience. Summarize your findings in a short paragraph.

2. How are camping evenings and nights different from your average run-of-the-mill evening? (See T-chart on next page)

Camping	Run-of-the-Mill
•No TV or other commercial entertainment	
•Storytelling	
•Different environmental sounds	

3. Sensory words and images in books: Brainstorm examples of sensory references in this book and other books. Prepare a word map or picture to summarize how authors appeal to the various senses.

Chapter 10—Pages 79-84

Plot Summary:
Brennan is mysteriously awakened from his sleep; he feels "something" amiss that he can't understand. Then he finds a human skull with a bullet hole in it. Though he thinks the action crazy, he puts the skull in his pack to take with him.

Discussion Questions:
1. Act out Brennan's awakening in Chapter 10. Is it a believable account? Why or why not?

Prediction:
Half the book lies ahead. What is going to happen? What is the skull? How are the two stories related and how will it all be resolved?

Chapter 11—Pages 87-95

Plot Summary:
Brennan takes no action regarding the skull, but he begins to have strange dreams in which he's doing and feeling things differently and beyond his experiences.

Vocabulary:
slewed 87   glowering 89   drenched 94
feigned 94

Discussion Questions:
1. What is Brennan's obsession in Chapter 11? *(the skull he found on the camping trip)* How is this obsession exhibited? *(He thinks about the skull a lot and also has strange unexplained dreams. He wonders if he is crazy.)*

2. What is the Mother Look? *(that concerned attention-focused quizzical expression mothers get when their children say new or unexplainable or troubling things)* Why does Brennan's mother give him the Mother Look? *(He asks if it was possible for crazy people to know they're going crazy.)* When has your mother used the Mother Look?

3. What is Brennan's decision at the end of Chapter 11? *(to find out about the skull)*

Chapter 12—Pages 97-99

Plot Summary:
Brennan ponders the skull some more and decides to consult Homesley.

Vocabulary:
    lope 99

Discussion Questions:
1. Why is Brennan starting to talk to himself, sometimes aloud? *(He has a problem he doesn't understand and is thinking hard about it.)*

2. What are some ways to make decisions? How does Brennan seem to make decisions? *(Answers vary, but may include the idea that he decides emotionally and intuitively.)*

Supplementary Activities:
1. Complete a decision-making chart, evaluating various solutions to Brennan's dilemma.

2. Investigate various decision-making schemes, such as IDEAL (identify, describe, evaluate, act, learn), pros and cons.

3. Classify the facts. What does Brennan know about the skull so far? What questions does he still have?

4. To explore sequencing, prepare single sentences or drawings on 3 x 5 cards to summarize various events in the story. Exchange with another classmate or group to challenge each other to put the cards in order. Brainstorm ways to put things in sequence. Create a class sequencing strategy chart.

Chapter 13—Pages 101-108

Plot Summary:
Brennan introduces John Homesley, his biology teacher. Homesley has interested Brennan in learning by introducing him to beetles.

Vocabulary:
> turret 104

Discussion Questions:

1. (Optional) Listen to Mahler's Resurrection Symphony. Brennan said the music was incredible. Record your thoughts as you listen. You may use narrative or pictorial.

2. Who is John Homesley? Answer with a listing of labels, as well as other ways the author has revealed the character.

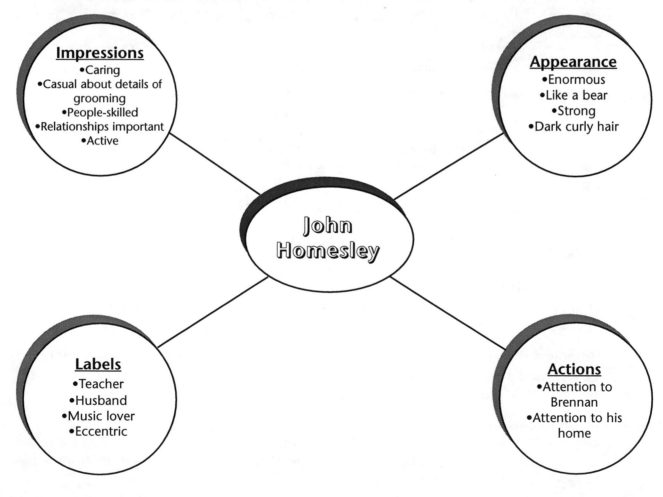

Impressions
- Caring
- Casual about details of grooming
- People-skilled
- Relationships important
- Active

Appearance
- Enormous
- Like a bear
- Strong
- Dark curly hair

John Homesley

Labels
- Teacher
- Husband
- Music lover
- Eccentric

Actions
- Attention to Brennan
- Attention to his home

3. Is John Homesley a good choice for help? Why?

Chapter 14—Pages 111-115

Plot Summary:
Homesley reacts calmly to Brennan's revelation about the skull he found in Dog Canyon, speculating about it.

Vocabulary:

medic 113	constitute 113	nonexistent 113
surmise 114	speculate 114	pathology 114
morgue 115		

Discussion Questions:
1. How does Homesley puzzle through problems? *(As a scientist, he evaluates the evidence piece by piece and considers various possible options. His working mode is to walk back and forth.)*

2. Why doesn't a voice in his mind tell Brennan what to do? *(Answers vary.)*

Chapter 15—Pages 117-121

Plot Summary:
Tibbets examines the skull and identifies it as that of a fourteen-year-old Indian boy who died violently with a large bore rifle shot by someone else.

Vocabulary:

scalpel 117	corpse 118	calipers 119
bore 120	muzzle 120	self-inflicted 120
reeled 121		

Discussion Questions:
1. Dramatize Tibbets' examination of the skull. What is his working method? *(quiet, precise, illustrating his thinking with a drawing)*

2. What is the "but" for Brennan at the end of the chapter? *(Answers vary—spirit of Coyote Runs.)* How does the author emphasize this part of the story? *(short direct sentences, positioned at the end of the chapter)*

Supplementary Activities:
1. Chapters 14 and 15 feature Homesley and Tibbets working. Brainstorm about different working modes with class members. Then investigate and *try out* different working styles.

2. Interview a teacher or principal about learning styles.

3. Writing: Homesley reminds me of _____. Brennan is _____.

4. How does an author choose names for characters? Are the names in *Canyons* appropriate? Why or why not? What are the best book character names you've read?

Chapter 16—Pages 123-127

Plot Summary:
Tibbets shares more suppositions about the skull and Homesley and Brennan decide to contact the Western Historical Archives for more information.

Vocabulary:

| Murphy drip 123 | caffeine 124 | stimulant 124 |
| archives 126 | | |

Discussion Questions:
1. What is a Murphy drip? *(Vietnam medic's use of concentrated coffee as a stimulant to combat shock)*

2. How do Homesley and Tibbets summarize Vietnam? *(Page 124, It was awful—"All of it...")*

3. Continue adding to the character webs. What information is added in this chapter? Are the characters flat or rounded? Flat characters are one-dimensional with limited development and one viewpoint. Rounded characters have greater development, change as the book proceeds and provide a broader picture.

Homesley: •*Has a variety of old friends, keeps up with old friends*
•*Was a medic in Vietnam and is willing to remember that time, but as something awful*

Brennan: •*Regrets about his father*
•*Impatient to gain more information*

4. Why haven't Homesley and Tibbets insisted or suggested that Brennan report or return the skull? *(Answers vary.)*

Chapter 17—Pages 129-132

Plot Summary:
Seven boxes of information arrive from Homesley's friend at the Western Historical Archives.

Discussion Questions:

1. How does Paulsen build up the anticipation in this chapter? *(He details Brennan's impatience before the boxes arrive and then gives details about the contents of the boxes and a brief quote from a newspaper account. He also provides a strong focus on the papers and finding the answer.)*

2. What is the point of view of the 1860's newspapers that Brennan reads? *(pro-settlers, anti-Indians)* Is that appropriate? Try writing a few headlines taking the Indian view-point.

Chapter 18—Pages 135-139

Plot Summary:
Brennan reads the archives' materials long into the night.

Vocabulary:
redundant 135	marauding 135	uprisings 136
hacked 136	cantina 137	prudent 137
arroyo 138	reeled 139	

Discussion Questions:

1. Why are the 1860's newspaper accounts so brutal? *(Answers vary—a brutal time after the Civil War, frontier justice, fewer court structures to deal with conflicts, and cultural clashes.)*

2. Have you ever stayed up very late investigating something? What gives you the capacity to stay aware? *(Answers vary—enthusiasm for discovery, or new materials to investigate.)*

Supplementary Activities:

1. Visit a historical collection or museum or interview an archivist. What kinds of things are included in archives?

2. Choose a historical period to create a fictional archives. Cooperative groups design things to include.

3. Using a small box or the cube pattern, put 3 small objects inside to typify Coyote Runs. Defend your choices. (See page 36 of this guide for cube pattern.)

4. Devise a word map or set of similes to give the flavor of the 1860s. Use the information from the book to guide your work.

Chapter 19—Pages 141-143

Plot Summary:
Brennan finds a patrol order and report which he believes identifies the skull.

Vocabulary:
skirmish 142   riffled 143

Discussion Questions:
1. Why is Brennan holding his breath when he reads the fateful patrol report? *(Answers vary. He is too excited to breathe.)*

2. Re-enact the chapter with one student reading aloud and other students taking the part of Brennan.

3. How does author Gary Paulsen hold your attention? *(Answers vary.)*

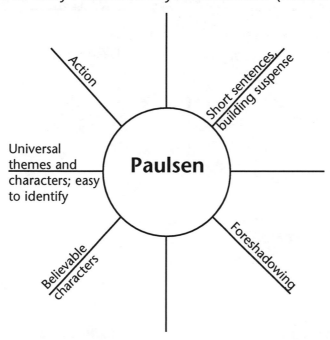

Chapter 20—Pages 145-150

Plot Summary:
Brennan discovers that the skull is all that remains of Coyote Runs, an Apache boy/man about the same age as Brennan when he was executed.

Vocabulary:

    retrieve 146   herbal tea 149

Discussion Questions:

1. What does Brennan learn from Amelia Gebhart's letter? Try to list as many bits of information as you can.

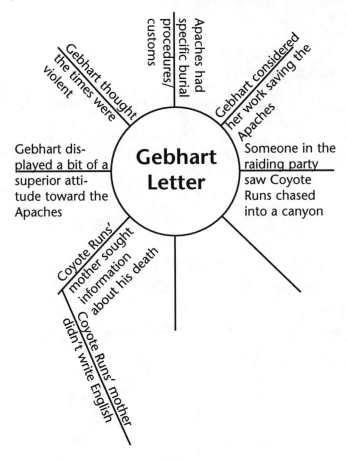

2. Why did Col. John McIntire lie? *(Answers vary—McIntire was protecting his soldiers. He didn't know the truth. He was embarrassed or feared reprisal if he told the truth.)*

3. What does Brennan understand as his mission in regards to the skull? *(He must return the skull to a proper burial place.)*

4. Reread the final paragraph of the chapter and predict how the story will end.

Chapter 21—Pages 153-156

Plot Summary:
Returning home, Brennan is confronted about the skull by his mother and Bill who have called the police. Brennan beats a quick retreat with the skull to return it to a burial place as the police arrive at the house.

Vocabulary:

prim 154   confiscate 155

Discussion Questions:
1. How do the various characters in the book react the first time they see/learn about the skull? *(Brennan—curiosity, bonding, connection; Homesley—thoughtful, pondering; Bill—primly, legally; Brennan's mother—with concern; Tibbets—clinically)* Which is the "right" reaction? Why?

2. Why does it say "time was gone" at the end of the chapter? *(Page 156, Brennan can't wait. He must bury the skull before it's confiscated and ends up as a museum exhibit.)*

Supplementary Activities:
1. Compare writing styles. To start, choose different examples from the book: Quaker letter, patrol order, newspaper accounts, Paulsen narrative. How do the styles vary? Consider point of view, kind of sentences, details given or omitted.

2. Complete a story map to summarize the story. Use a "standard story map" (page 32), or design your own "custom map."

Chapter 22—Pages 159-167

Plot Summary:
Brennan runs north to the canyons area on a quest to return the skull to a proper resting place. Once close to the canyons area, he sees and overhears his mother, Bill, Homesley, and a rescue party.

Vocabulary:

quills 162   sidewinder 162   buttes 164
warped 164   dehydration 167

Discussion Questions:
1. What is the significance of the words and sentences in italics? *(They are from Coyote Runs.)*

Story Map

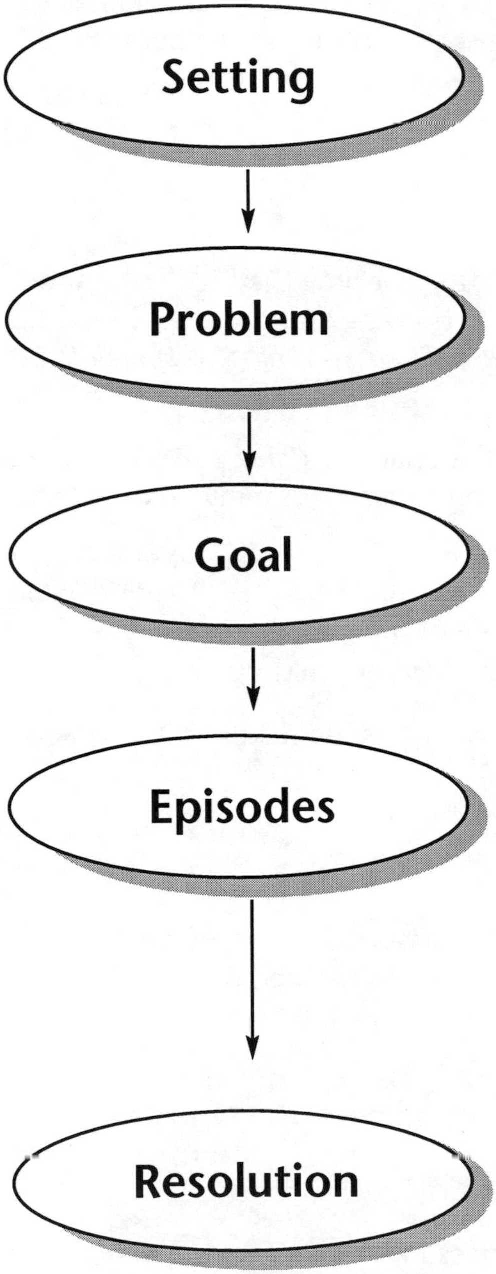

Characters_____

_____

_____

_____

Setting

↓

Problem

Time and Place_____

_____

_____

Goal

_____

_____

↓

Beginning ——→ Development ——→ Outcome

Episodes

_____

_____

_____

_____

↓

_____

_____

Resolution

_____

_____

_____

2. How can you explain the communication between Coyote Runs and Brennan? *(Answers vary. It is somewhat beyond explanation. It is in a novel and could be fantasy.)*

3. How might this story be considered a quest story? In a quest story, the hero has a mission of some sort to accomplish. What other quest adventures have you read? How is *Canyons* similar to those books?

Chapter 23—Pages 169-173

Plot Summary:
Brennan is spotted by the rescue party, but, encouraged by his mother, Brennan breaks free. In a strange twist, he feels a pain similar to the one Coyote Runs encountered when he was shot in the ankle.

Vocabulary:

windmilled 171   loping 171   exulted 171

Discussion Questions:
1. Re-enact the confrontation between Brennan and the rescue team.

2. Why does his mother change her mind and tell Brennan to run? *(Answers vary. She comes to understand Brennan's quest.)*

3. How do the rescue men and cavalry soldiers get mixed up? *(Brennan is being pursued by the rescue men as Coyote Runs was chased by cavalry soldiers. It's part of the similarities between the two boys throughout the book.)*

Chapter 24—Pages 175-184

Plot Summary:
Brennan takes the skull to the medicine place where the spirit of Coyote Runs is set free.

Vocabulary:

urgency 177   fissure 179   weathered 179
butte 182

Discussion Questions:
1. What is the significance of the repetition of the word "up"? *(On page 15, Paulsen alludes to the Apache medicine place and heavenward being high and away. Also Brennan is climbing up.)*

2. What is set free at the end of the book? *(The spirit of Coyote Runs and Brennan lost the strange compelling draw from the skull. The quest is completed.)*

Culminating Activities:

1. Choose 5 scenes from the book as suggestions for an illustrator. Defend your choices.

2. Cast the movie *Canyons*. (See page 35 of this guide.)

3. Complete the K-W-L chart, filling in the last column to summarize what you've learned of nineteenth century Apaches and the El Paso, Texas area. Add an extra column for questions you still have.

4. Devise Brennan's "What I Did On My Summer Vacation" essay.

5. Create a letter to the Denver officials to offer thanks and to share the outcome.

6. Complete the story map to summarize the story.

7. "Gary Paulsen has created a well-crafted story in *Canyons*." Agree or disagree. Support your answer.

8. What are the author's main ideas and themes in *Canyons*?

9. What did the character of Brennan learn in the book? How did the character change from the beginning to the end of the book?

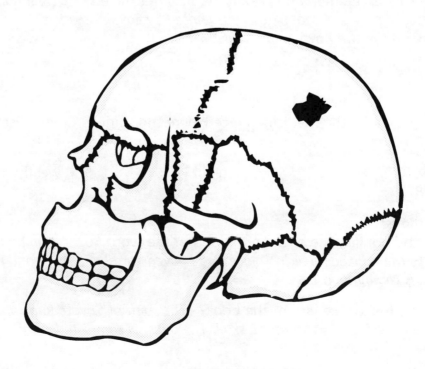

Your Book Has Been Optioned for the Movies

1. You are the casting director. Who are the lead roles, supporting cast, and walk-ons? What kind of characters are they? What actors will fill the rolls? How should they look? What acting abilities will they need?

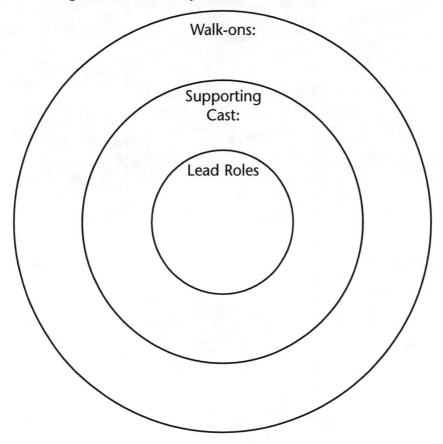

Walk-ons:

Supporting
Cast:

Lead Roles

2. Design costumes for the cast. Explain your choices.

3. Pick the music. Will you need background music only or will you have musical "numbers"?

4. Design the set.

5. Identify and describe the props.

6. What will you title your movie? Why?

Character Cube

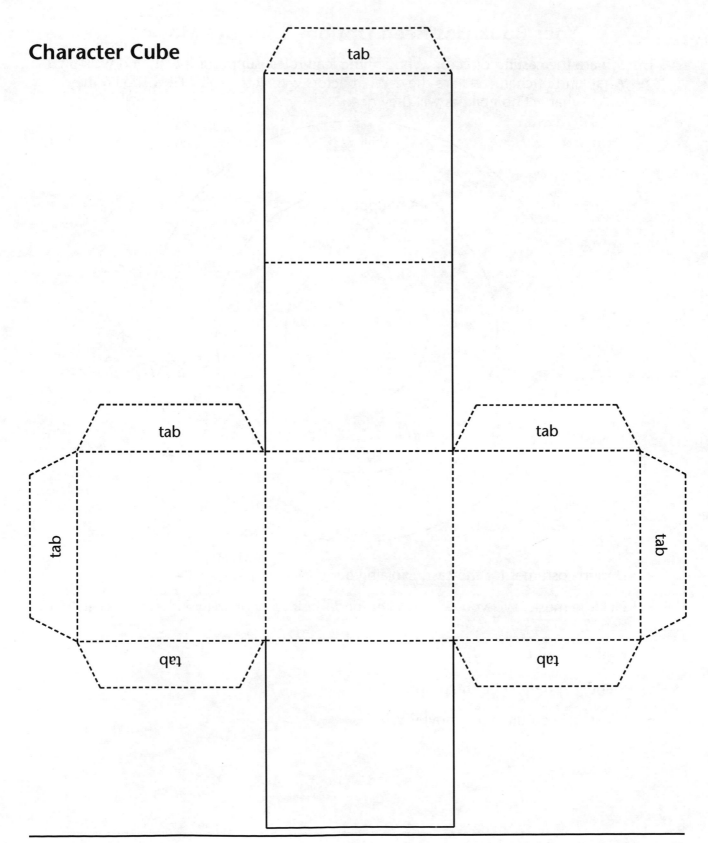

© Novel Units, Inc.